the two MUTCH SISTERS

Words by **Carol Brendler**

Art by **Lisa Brown**

CLARION BOOKS

HOUGHTON MIFFLIN HARCOURT

Boston   New York

The **MUTCH SISTERS** were collectors.

It started when they were very little girls.

First there were two toy teapots.

One for Ruby,

one for Violet.

As the sisters grew,
so did their collection . . .

Two sundials,

    two snorkels,

two bouffant wigs,

two whirligigs

. . . until the house they shared was stuffed to the shingles
with two of everything!
Two clavichords, two birch canoes,
two tapestries, two skeps for bees.

Drawers bulged.
Cupboards wouldn't close.
The two Mutch sisters
had too much stuff!

There was no place to set
their teacups during teatime.

Violet Mutch was perfectly
content to hold her
teacup on her lap.

Ruby Mutch

was not.

"I've had enough!" said Ruby to Violet.
"This house isn't big enough for the both of us.
I'm moving out."

"You wouldn't," said Violet, her teacup rattling.

"Oh, yes, I would," Ruby said.

And Ruby did. She packed up her half of their collection.

One gargoyle,

one glockenspiel,

one brass spittoon

. . . one French bassoon.

"You shouldn't," said Violet, her voice trembling.

"Oh, yes, I should," said Ruby. "And I shall."

While Violet looked on,
Ruby loaded half of everything
onto a truck.

One crinoline,
one paper kite,
one fireplug,
one bearskin rug.

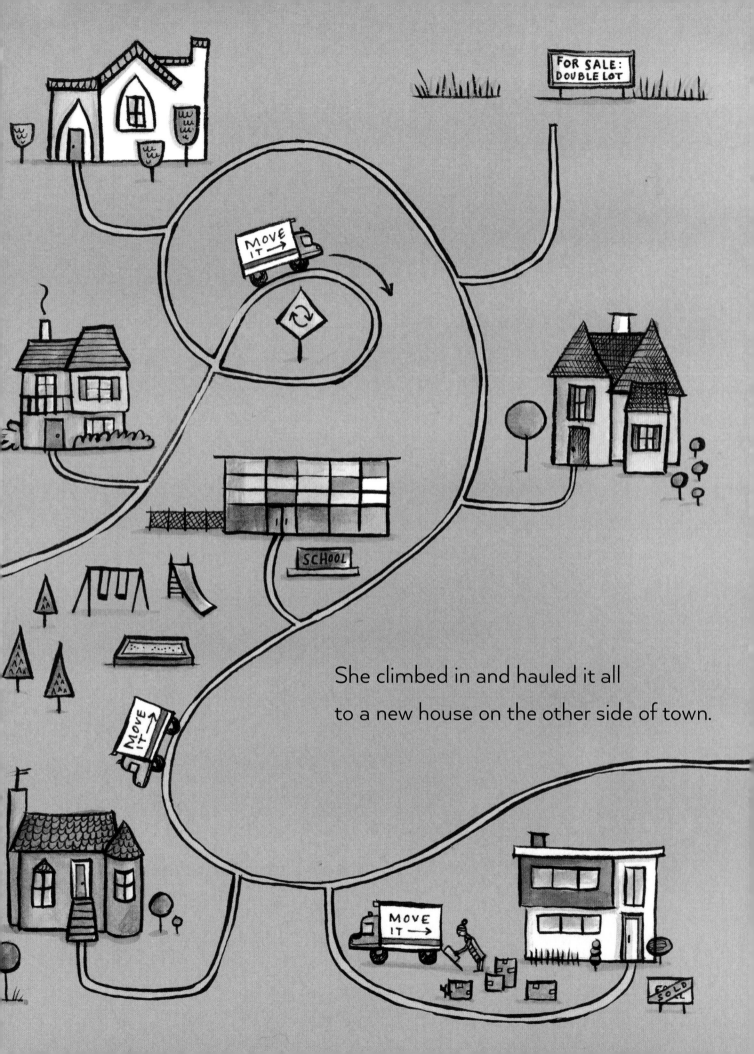

She climbed in and hauled it all
to a new house on the other side of town.

Ruby arranged everything to her liking.

Violet visited and brought Ruby
a housewarming gift.

"Neither one of us has too much now,"
announced Ruby.
"I have made everything just right."

"You haven't," said Violet, toppling her teacup.

"Oh, yes, I have," said Ruby. "And I like it."

Ruby tidied her collection every day,
displaying each object to its best advantage.

A rowing oar,
one fuzzy die,
a swimming fin,
a moccasin.

But something was missing, Ruby thought.

Violet thought so too.

Ruby hadn't the slightest idea
what it could be.

But Violet knew.

The next day,
Violet's collection disappeared.

And so did Violet.

Days passed.

Ruby worried.

Then one day,
she spotted Violet out front.

Violet Mutch had come back,
and with her came . . .

pneumatic jacks,
a stack of sleds,
a chest of tools,
a pack of mules.

"You won't," Ruby said.

"Oh, yes, I will," said Violet.

Up went Ruby's new house.

Underneath went the sleds.

The mules were hitched, and . . .

"HYAW!" cried Violet.

What a sight!

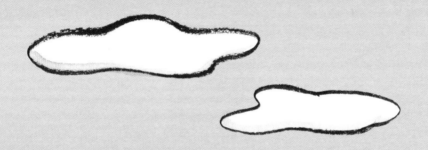

Violet Mutch plunked Ruby's house down right next to hers.

"You didn't!" said Ruby.

"I DID!"

said Violet.

"Just look. Two sisters. Two houses. And now that you're near, dear, nothing is missing."

From that day on, the two Mutch sisters
never had too much of anything.

They had each other close by . . .

and that was just enough.

For my sister, Lisa—C.B.

In memory of Jack Brown,
my favorite pack rat—L.B.

Clarion Books
3 Park Avenue
New York, New York 10016

Text copyright © 2018 by Carol Brendler
Illustrations copyright © 2018 by Lisa Brown

Clarion Books is an imprint of Houghton Mifflin Harcourt Publishing Company.

hmhco.com

The illustrations in this book were done in India ink and watercolor on paper.

The text was set in Arquitecta Book.

Library of Congress Cataloging-in-Publication Data
Names: Brendler, Carol, author. | Brown, Lisa, 1972- illustrator.
Title: The two Mutch sisters / words by Carol Brendler ; art by Lisa Brown.
Description: Boston ; New York : Clarion Books, Houghton Mifflin Harcourt,
[2018] | Summary: Ruby and Violet Mutch, a matched pair, have always
collected things in pairs, but when their house will no longer hold
everything, Ruby packs her things and moves out.
Identifiers: LCCN 2016049420 | ISBN 9780544430747 (hardcover)
Subjects: | CYAC: Sisters—Fiction. | Collectors and collecting—Fiction.
Classification: LCC PZ7.B7512 Two 2018 | DDC [E]—dc23
LC record available at https://lccn.loc.gov/2016049420

Manufactured in China
SCP 10 9 8 7 6 5 4 3 2 1
4500689134